S0-AGB-403

THE JONES FAMILY EXPRESS

Postcard 1 (top right, address side)

Steven
18282 St Marks are
Brooklyn NY 11288

Do not write below this line

Postcard 2 (top, message)

the wind it is
rough! The people
here say this is
normal How can I
believe this ha ha ha
Love Carolyn

Photo: Karina Wang, IL

Postcard 3 (top left fragment)

... if you turn
... it looks
... doesn't
... Boy oh Boy
... umidity is
... Auntie Carolyn

Steven
18282 St Marks are
Brooklyn NY 11288

Do not write below this line

Postcard (top right, tilted)

...gton D.C. is
... little town
... very quiet
... man
... to see
... blay hunt
... aunt

Steven
18282 St Marks are
Brooklyn NY 11288

Published by: L.B. Prince Co.. Fairfax, VA.

...ox 221, Glencoe, IL 60022 Tel (847) 835-2941

Center postcard (COLUMBIA)

COLUMBIA

Photo © Sid Tra...

...arbor is
...filled
...cury

... it tried this soup
it is so good!, I wish
you could try it. Aunt Carolyn

Brooklyn

BEENTHERE
SAWTHAT
Virtually Everywhere!

...Company, Baltimore, MD (800...

DO NOT WRITE BELOW THIS LINE

Steven
18282 St Marks a...
Brooklyn NY 11298

Left postcard (Cambridge Portfolio)

The
CAMBRIDGE
PORTFOLIO

Hello Steven
London is very
humid today
I & humid today
lovely I wish
... already
...

Steven
18282 St. Marks are
Brooklyn NY 11288

ST JOHN'S COLLEGE
...RAWLE ©
...and may not be reproduced in any form without permission
Ref PC56

Florida Seasons postcard (right)

Spring
Winter
Florida Seasons

Bottom center postcard

FLORIDA IMPRESSIONS
SUPER CARD

Arts Inc
oro, SC 29...

The pla...
appearance...
has made it a figure of the...
It is a distant relative of the...
from the air and merely uses the...

Hi Steven
...
St. Marks A...

Steven

... in shops
of the
...ould

Bottom right postcard (Cape May)

CAPE MAY SCENICS
A Day At The Beach
Another gorgeous beach day at America's grandest family
resort, Cape May, N.J.
Photo: Jim McWilliams

Hey Steven
I am at the
... a lot

Steven
18282 St...

3111 RT. 38 # 11 - SUITE 106
9054 · ☎ (609) 829-4181

Stamps

ПОЧТА СССР 16к + 6к 1979 Игра XXII Олимпиада Москва 80

ПОЧТА СССР 4к + 2к Игры XXI олимпиады 1976

ПОЧТА СССР 6к Игры XXI олимпиады 1976

Postcard 1 (top left):
that the cotton pickers
would put rocks in
the cotton so that
it would weigh
more!
Love Carolyn

© and Pub. by Photo Arts, Inc.

PLEASE DO NOT WRITE BELOW THIS LINE. SPACE RESERVED FOR U.S. POSTAL SERVICE.

Steven Jones
18282 St. Marks ave
Brooklyn NY 11288

Postcard (top right):
Washington Monument at Sunset. Washington, D.C.
Published by: L.B. Prince Co., Fairfax, VA.
Photo by: Bob Anderson

Street and Chrysler
Brooklyn, NY 11288
18282 St. Marks ave

Postcard (Buttermilk Falls):
© SCENIC DESIGNS, INC. – 1401 INDUSTRIAL HWY. – (856) 829-4181
CINNAMINSON, NJ 08077

View More Great Photography Online!
www.BeenThereSawThat.com/NJ

BUTTERMILK FALLS
Kittatinny Mountains, New Jersey
The falls can be reached via the Appalachian Trail or by
dirt road within the Delaware Water Gap Recreation Area.
The best time to visit is in April/May when the falls are at
their fullest.
Photo: Gene Ahrens

Postcard (CHI 226):
CHI 226
The Water Tower, Water Tower Place and
John Hancock Center.

Steven
Went to this tower
and purchase, many
things. Some of the
items are for you
because I know you
would it be here.

PHOTOS by 221, Glencoe, IL 60022 Tel (847) 835-2941

Postcard (PHOTOSCAPES):
PHOTOSCAPES® P.O. Box 221, Glencoe, IL 60022 Tel (847) 835-2941

Steven
18282 St. Marks a
Brooklyn NY 112

Envelope (bottom center):
Steven
18282 St. Marks ave
Brooklyn NY 11288

Traub Company · Baltimore, MD (800) 933-2220
Post

Photos © Sid Traub

Postcard (bottom):
The main attraction along
Photo by Florida Air Shots

CHESAPEAKE BAY
...000 miles of shoreline, the Chesapeake, the largest inland estuary. A century ago, this was
by far the nation's best-lit waterway. The earlier lighthouses
were conical stone structures, but the vicious shoals of the
bay required screw-pile construction which engineers
developed by the 1850's.

MISS Selfr...
Islington

To Georgette Jones, my Uncle Charles Steptoe, and
the Steptoe, Douglas, and Hill families—my family

—J.S.

Text and illustrations copyright © 2003 by Javaka Steptoe

All rights reserved. No part of the contents of this book may be reproduced
by any means without the written permission of the publisher.

LEE & LOW BOOKS Inc., 95 Madison Avenue, New York, NY 10016
leeandlow.com

Many thanks to Colin Channer for his help with this project.

Manufactured in China

Book design by Christy Hale
Book production by The Kids at Our House
Art photography by Gamma One Conversions, New York City

The text is set in Lemonade Bold
The illustrations are rendered in cut paper and mixed-media collage

(HC)   10   9   8   7   6   5   4   3   2
(PB)   10   9   8   7   6   5   4   3   2   1
First Edition

Library of Congress Cataloging-in-Publication Data
Steptoe, Javaka.
The Jones family express/ Javaka Steptoe.– 1st ed.
p. cm.
Summary: Steven tries to find just the right present for Aunt Carolyn in time for
the annual block party.
ISBN 1-58430-047-7 (hardcover)   ISBN 1-58430-262-3 (paperback)
[1. Gifts–Fiction. 2. Aunts–Fiction. 3. Parties–Fiction. 4. African Americans–Fiction.] I. Title.
PZ7.S83668 Jo 2003   [Fic]–dc21   2002067120

ISBN-13: 978-1-58430-047-2 (hardcover)   ISBN-13: 978-1-58430-262-9 (paperback)

THE JONES FAMILY EXPRESS

Javaka Steptoe

Lee & Low Books Inc. • New York

Every summer for as long as I can remember, my Aunt Carolyn has gone traveling. Sometimes she would go out of the country and other times she just got on a train and visited different places. She always had funny stories to tell when she returned.

I thought Aunt Carolyn's stories were so much fun that once, when I was three, I hid in her suitcase so she would take me with her. She was so tickled, she promised to send me a postcard from every place she went until I was old enough to travel with her. Grandma had to read the postcards to me at first, but as I got older, I read them myself.

Those postcards always made me feel special.

This summer Aunt Carolyn said she would be here for our annual block party. The block party was my favorite time of the year because the whole family visited us at Grandma's house. People came from everywhere, and there was a lot of food, music, and things to do. Aunt Carolyn didn't come back often, so I wanted to get something special for her. I just didn't know what.

The night before the party, I barely got any sleep. My cousin Sean was staying over, and I had to share my bed with him. Sean was always asking questions.

"Why do dogs like dog biscuits?" he asked.

"I don't know," I answered, but I wasn't really listening. I just lay there thinking until I came up with an idea. Maybe I could find something for Aunt Carolyn on Nostrand Avenue! You can buy almost anything there.

The next morning I woke up to the smell of Grandma's pancakes.

"Get up, Sean," I said, poking him in his ribs. "It's time to get up!" We got dressed and ran downstairs.

"Good morning, Grandma," we sang as we sat down to heaping plates of her buttery-syrupy pancakes.

Uncle Charles walked in, grumpy as usual. Sean and I covered our plates with our arms because Uncle Charles liked to take bites of your food.

"Stop it, Charles," Grandma said just as he reached for one of my pancakes.

"I only do it out of love," Uncle Charles replied, acting all innocent. "I want to make sure it's not poisoned."

In between bites Sean told Grandma how he'd been working on a rap for the block party talent show.

Suddenly the phone rang.

"Hey, Carolyn," Grandma said in her cheery voice. "When are you getting in?... The 2:30 train? You need anything?... All right then, we'll see you soon."

I looked at my watch. I had only about four and a half hours until Aunt Carolyn arrived!

Just then Aunt Marsha walked in carrying three big bags of potatoes.

I looked at Sean. "We better get out of here before they have us peeling potatoes," I whispered.

When we reached the vestibule door, we heard country music blasting. That could mean only one thing. Granddad! I didn't want to get trapped having to help Granddad make his secret barbecue sauce that everybody knew the secret to. Besides, Granddad liked to tell long stories.

"Sean," I said. "Go talk to Granddad. I'll be out in a minute."

As soon as Sean was gone, I ran up to my room, climbed out the window onto our neighbor's toolshed, and made my way past her garden to the street. Then I headed toward Nostrand Avenue.

The first place I went was Perkins Drugstore. The store had shelves and shelves of stuff. I wandered up and down the aisles, picking up things, until I heard someone come up behind me.

"How may I help you, young maaaaan?" I cringed. It was Mr. Perkins, the owner. He had the screechiest voice ever. It was like nails scratching on a chalkboard.

I told him I wanted to find a special gift for my favorite aunt.

"What about some caaards?" Mr. Perkins said. "Or we have delicious chocolaaaates. She might like some perfuuuume."

I shook my head no, so he started suggesting other things. I listened politely until my head started to hurt.

"Thank you," I said finally. "Let me think about it some more." Then I walked quickly out of the store, rubbing my ears.

Next I went to Ms. Ruby's shop. She's from Jamaica. She had lots of handmade things in her store, and I loved the way she talked.

"Hey, sweetie. How you do?" Ms. Ruby asked.

"I'm looking for a surprise for my Aunt Carolyn," I answered, looking around the shop. "I've saved up ten dollars and seventy-five cents."

"Okay," Ms. Ruby said. "She must be really special. You see anything you might like?"

"What about that picture frame?" I said. "Aunt Carolyn loves elephants."

"That one kinda expensive," she said. "It cost twenty-seven dollars."

I put on my best smile and told her I was a little short.

"You short for true," she said, and chuckled. "If you did have a likkle more money, I woulda sell it to you. But sorry, m'love. The money too short. You see a next one that you like?"

I looked around but didn't see anything else.

"No, thank you," I said. I left Ms. Ruby's feeling a little down.

As I left the store, I saw Uncle Charles walking toward me. I tried to hide, but he had already spotted me.

"Where have you been, Steven?" Uncle Charles asked. "It's almost time for the block party."

Uncle Charles knew how to fix all sorts of things, but he wouldn't do anything unless you paid him. Not even for kids. He was my last chance, though.

"I've been looking for a present for Aunt Carolyn," I explained. "Ms. Ruby's shop is too expensive, and there's nothing special enough at Perkins's."

"Come with me," Uncle Charles said. "I've got just the thing. How much money do you have?"

"Ten dollars," I said. I kept the seventy-five cents for myself. I couldn't let him take all my money!

We went to Uncle Charles's house, which was pretty junky. He had some of everything there—bike parts, old toys, magazines, radios, VCRs, you name it.

Uncle Charles started rummaging around his apartment, looking for things that might be useful. Every few minutes he would hold up something weird.

"What about this?" Uncle Charles would ask.

I would shake my head no.

"You've got to give me some help here," Uncle Charles complained after I said no to several things. So I started digging around. All of a sudden, there it was, the perfect thing.

"Look at this!" I said, holding up a big toy train. It needed a lot of fixing up—the paint was peeling off and some of the windows were broken, but I could see it had potential. I got busy right away. I had to work fast if I was going to finish in time to meet Aunt Carolyn at the train station.

I arrived at the station just as the train was coming in. A big crowd of people rushed down the stairs toward me. After almost everybody had left the station, I spotted Aunt Carolyn.

"Hey, Steven!" Aunt Carolyn called. She bustled over and plopped down her bags. She gave me a big kiss, and I gave her a nice, big hug.

"How's my little man doing?" Aunt Carolyn said. "Oh! You've gotten so big and handsome. I don't know who's more handsome now, you or Sean."

"Me of course!" I said, and we both just laughed.

"So what do you have there, Steven?" Aunt Carolyn asked, pointing to the package under my arm.

"It's a surprise for you," I said as I handed her the package.

Without saying a word, Aunt Carolyn opened her gift. As soon as she got the wrapping off, she put the train up to her face and turned it around and around.

"Steven," Aunt Carolyn said, and gave a big laugh. "This is the best present anyone has ever given me!"

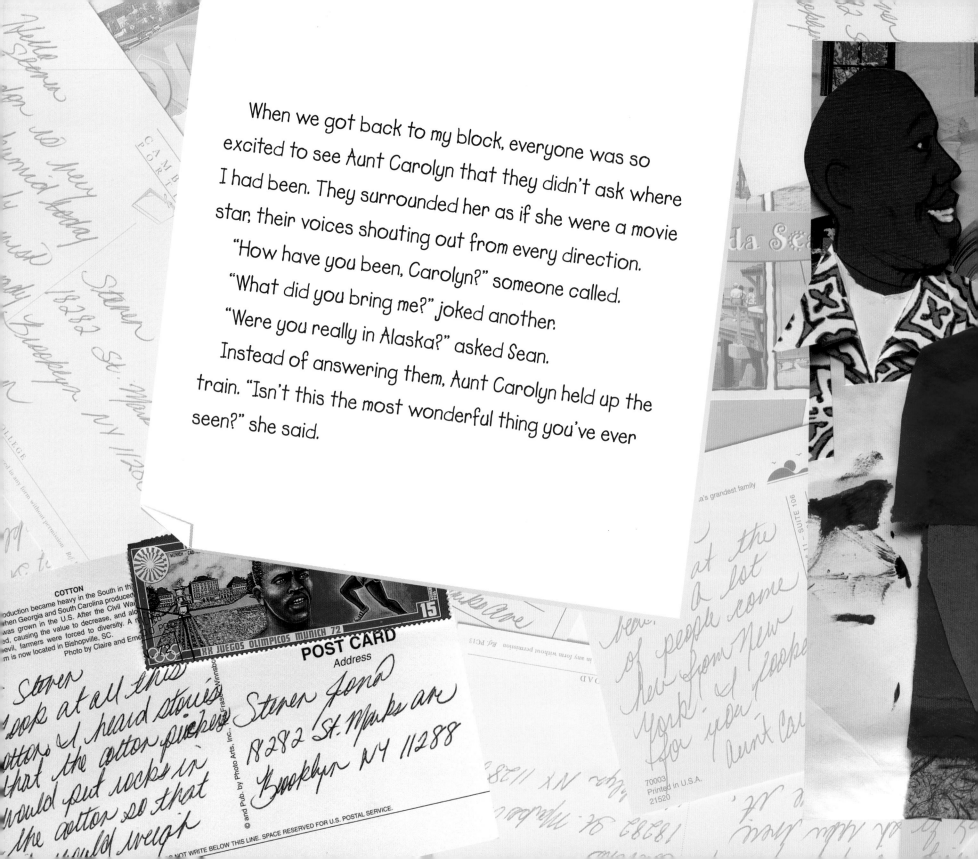

When we got back to my block, everyone was so excited to see Aunt Carolyn that they didn't ask where I had been. They surrounded her as if she were a movie star, their voices shouting out from every direction.

"How have you been, Carolyn?" someone called.

"What did you bring me?" joked another.

"Were you really in Alaska?" asked Sean.

Instead of answering them, Aunt Carolyn held up the train. "Isn't this the most wonderful thing you've ever seen?" she said.

COTTON
...oduction became heavy in the South in th...
...when Georgia and South Carolina produced...
...was grown in the U.S. After the Civil Wa...
...ed, causing the value to decrease, and alo...
...evil, farmers were forced to diversity. A...
...m is now located in Bishopville, SC.
Photo by Claire and Ern...

XX JUEGOS OLIMPICOS MUNICH 72   15

POST CARD
Address

Steven Jones
8282 St. Marks ave
Brooklyn NY 11288

© and Pub. by Photo Arts, Inc.

...DO NOT WRITE BELOW THIS LINE. SPACE RESERVED FOR U.S. POSTAL SERVICE.

70003
Printed in U.S.A.
21520

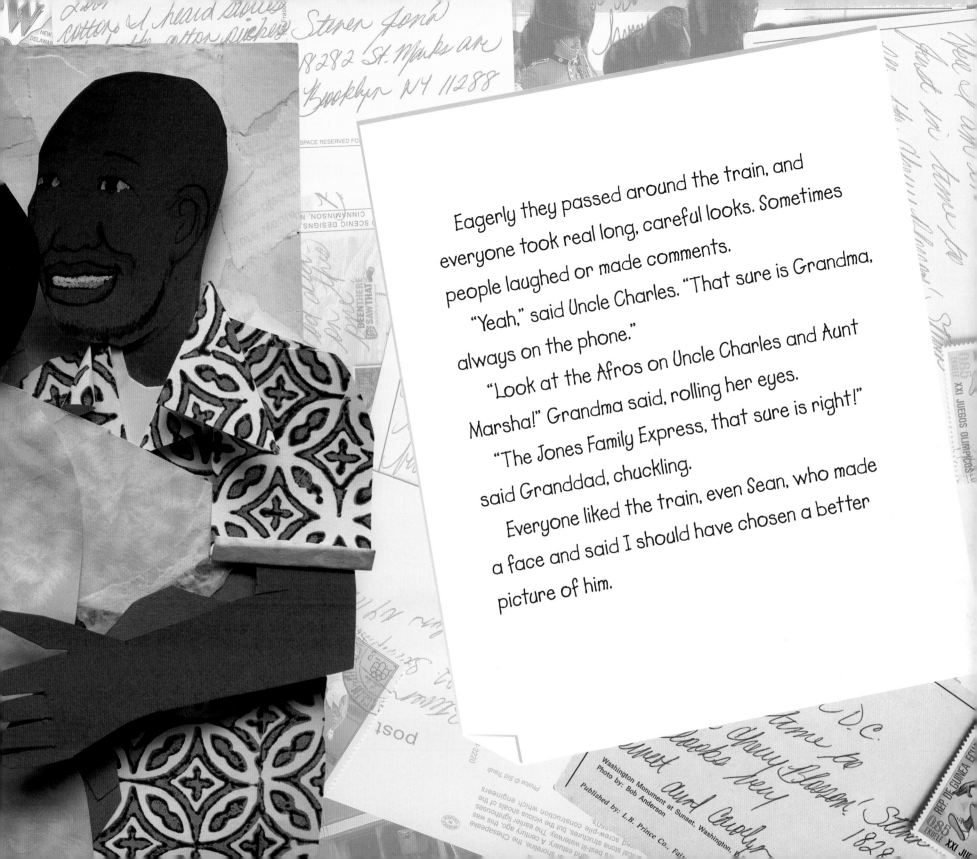

Eagerly they passed around the train, and everyone took real long, careful looks. Sometimes people laughed or made comments.

"Yeah," said Uncle Charles. "That sure is Grandma, always on the phone."

"Look at the Afros on Uncle Charles and Aunt Marsha!" Grandma said, rolling her eyes.

"The Jones Family Express, that sure is right!" said Granddad, chuckling.

Everyone liked the train, even Sean, who made a face and said I should have chosen a better picture of him.

The rest of the day flew by. Aunt Carolyn put her train on an old cake stand in the kitchen window where everyone could see it.

Granddad cooked his best batch of barbecue ever. There were so many greasy barbecue-stained little kids running around that it looked as if they had been in a mud fight. Sean actually won the rap contest. The band liked him so much, they let him be a special guest DJ until it was time to pack up the music. The most surprising thing of all was that Uncle Charles bought ice cream for everybody with my ten dollars and didn't try to eat anyone else's but his own.

The JONES FAMILY EXPRESS

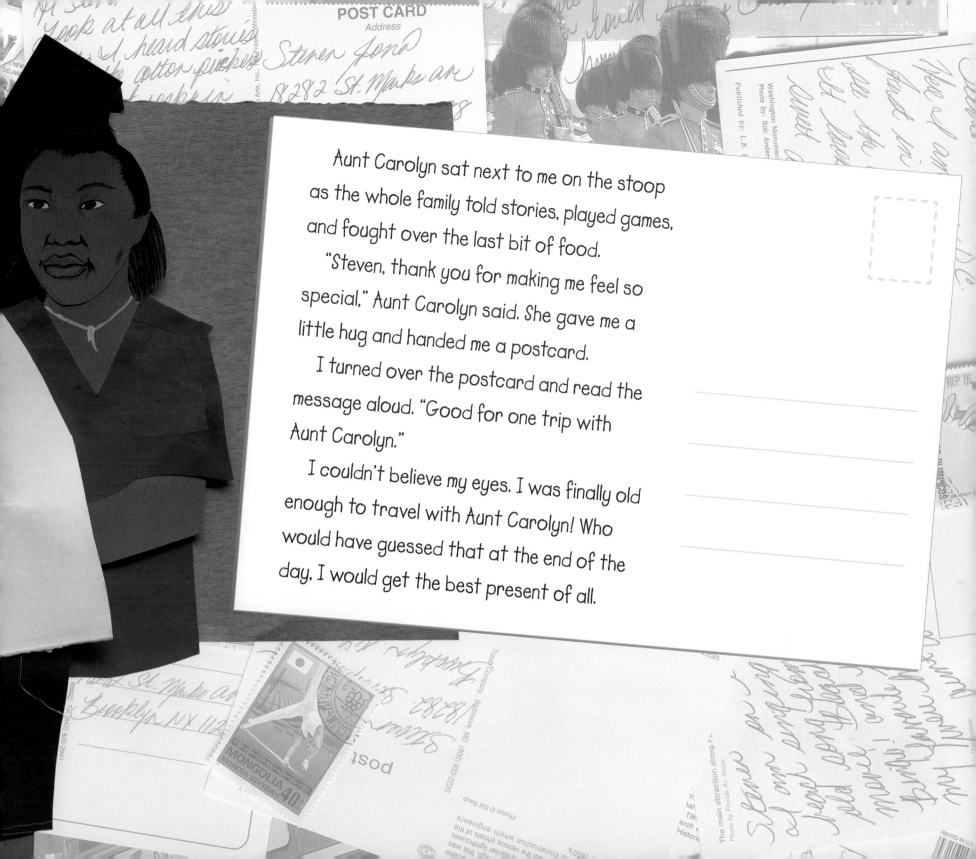

POST CARD
Address

Aunt Carolyn sat next to me on the stoop as the whole family told stories, played games, and fought over the last bit of food.

"Steven, thank you for making me feel so special," Aunt Carolyn said. She gave me a little hug and handed me a postcard.

I turned over the postcard and read the message aloud. "Good for one trip with Aunt Carolyn."

I couldn't believe my eyes. I was finally old enough to travel with Aunt Carolyn! Who would have guessed that at the end of the day, I would get the best present of all.

BEEN THERE
SAW THAT
Virtually Everywhere!

The Cambridge
PORTFOLIO

Steven
18282 St. Marks Av
Brooklyn NY 11298

Company, Baltimore, MD (800...

FLORIDA IMPRESSIONS
· SUPER CARD ·

Florida Seasons

Winter

Post Card

SPANISH MOSS IN THE CAROLINA LOW-COUNTRY
from the air and merely uses the tree as an anchor.
It is a distant relative of the pineapple, draws its sustenance
has made it a figure of legends, poems, and old wives' tales.
appearance, haunting by moonlight and evocative by day,
The plant, neither Spanish nor moss, because of its ethereal

Photo by Ernest Ferguson

Arts, Inc.
oro. SC 29180

...ANA ISLANDS

SO
CA

CAPE MAY SCENICS
A Day At The Beach
Another gorgeous beach day at America's grandest family
resort, Cape May, N.J.
Photo: Jim McWilliams

Hey Steven
I am at the
beach. A lot
of people come
here from New
York. I looked
for you.
Aunt Carolyn

Steven
18282 St. N...
Brook...

© SCENIC DESIGNS, INC. – 3111 RT. 38 # 11 – SUITE 106
MT. LAUREL, NJ 08054 – (609) 829-4181

70003
Printed in U.S.A.
21520

Steven
18282 St. Marks Ave
Brooklyn NY 11288

Ref: PC13
in any form without permission.

Savannah River
Plant
U.S. Atomic Energy
Commission
Reservation

Allendale

Lake
Moultrie

Georgetown

Cooper
River

Cypress
Gardens

321

Things. Some of the items are for you because I know you...it be here!

©SPI

View More Great...
BeenThe...

BUTTERMILK FALLS, Ne...
Kittatinny Mountains,...
The falls can be reached...
dirt road within the Dela...
The best time to visit is i...
their fullest.
Photo: Gene Ahrens

XXI JUEGOS OLIMPICOS

ПОЧТА CCCP 1991 20k

60 MONGOLIA МОНГОЛ ШУУДАН

MONGOLIA 40н МОНГОЛ ШУУДАН

MONGOLIA 30 МОНГОЛ ШУУДАН

PHOTOSCAPES™ P.O. Box 221, Glencoe, IL 60022 Tel (847) 835-2941

Steven
18282 St. Marks A...
Brooklyn NY 112...

post

Traub Company, Baltimore, MD (800) 933-2220
Photos © Sid Traub

PRINTED IN CANADA

CHESAPEAKE BAY
With more than 4,000 miles of shoreline, the Chesapeake
is America's largest inland estuary. A century ago, this was
by far the nation's best-lit waterway. The earlier lighthouses
were conical stone structures, but the vicious shoals of the
bay required screw-pile construction which engineers
developed by the 1850's.

MD27

The main attraction along F...
Photo by Florida Air Shots

Miss Selfri...

King's Cross   Islington
Euston

...HAM FOUNTAIN
...icago
...go's Grant Park, Buckingham
...regularly visited attractions of
Photo © D. Maenza

Steve...
18282 St...
Brooklyn...

PHIL MATTES
POST CARD SHOPPE

Steven
There is nothing like
riding a convertible
down this road.
At least that is
what they say! Because
Lord knows I don't know...

Steven
18282 St. Marks ave
Brooklyn NY 11288

MIAMI BEACH
THE RESORT CITY
...ainbleu Hotel along Collins Avenue, you can

By Tristar Sales, Inc.
Bessemer, AL 35022 800-656-57...

MONTREAL

0 42768 41